Cultures of the World!

Saudi Arabia, Israel & Iran

Culture for Kids

Children's Cultural Studies Books

PROFESSOR GUSTO

EDUCATIONAL & INFORMATIVE BOOKS FOR CHILDREN
(PRE-K / K-12)

What do you know about Saudi Arabia, Israel and Iran? What do they have in common?

Read on and learn their interesting beliefs and practices.

Culture of Saudi Arabia

The Arabian culture is characterized by the Arabic language and Islam. The society is known to be religious, conservative, traditional and family oriented

Limitations on behavior and dress are strictly implemented. This is to follow the principle of encouraging good behavior and discouraging anything not traditional.

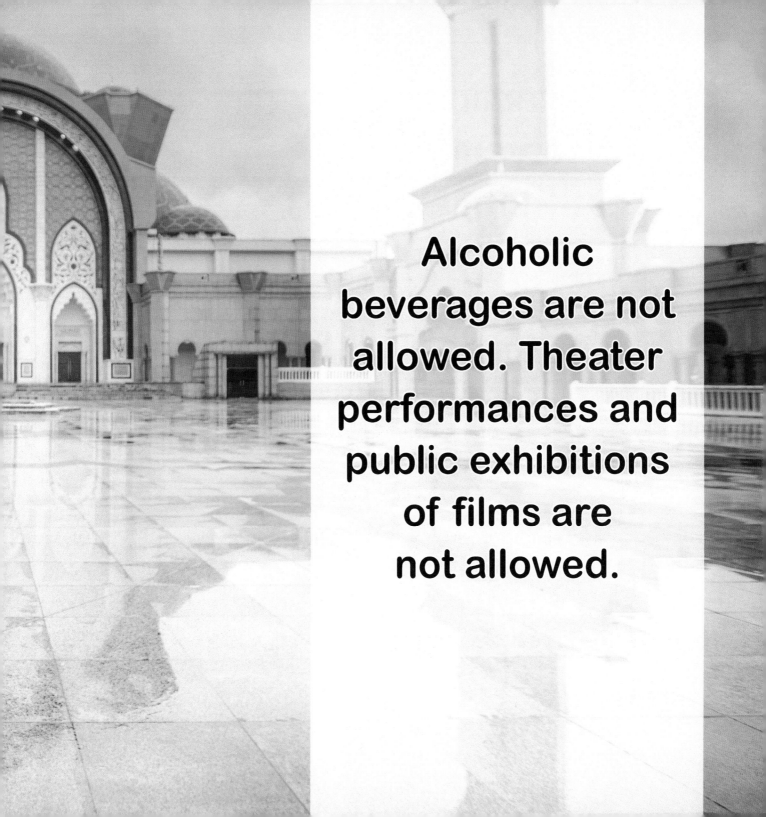

Alcoholic beverages are not allowed. Theater performances and public exhibitions of films are not allowed.

Islamic observances greatly influence the pattern of daily life. Muslims are called to pray five times each day. Their weekend is Friday and Saturday. This is because Friday is the holiest day for Muslims.

Culture
of Israel

Israel is the only Jewish state in the world. Immigration of Jews from all over the world shaped the composition of the population. Freedom of worship is allowed.

Most of the holidays celebrated in Israel are the same as the holidays observed by Jews all over the world.

Israel is an ancient country in the Middle East. It is bordered by the Mediterranean Sea, Lebanon, Palestine, Jordan and Egypt.

Three western religions claim Israel. For example, Jerusalem and Galilee are considered sacred among Christians. The Jews believe that Messiah will come to Israel. Muslims believe that Muhammad went up to heaven from Jerusalem.

Culture
of Iran

Most Iranians practice Islam. It governs their personal, political, economic and legal lives.

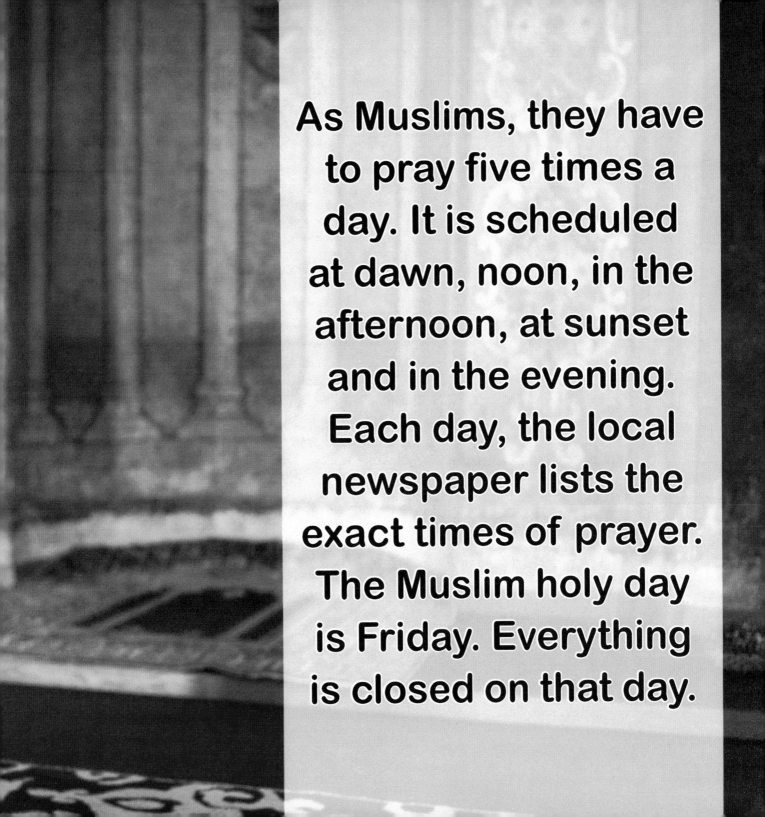

As Muslims, they have to pray five times a day. It is scheduled at dawn, noon, in the afternoon, at sunset and in the evening. Each day, the local newspaper lists the exact times of prayer. The Muslim holy day is Friday. Everything is closed on that day.

During Ramadan, a month of prayer and fasting, families and friends gather together each night at sunset to celebrate the breaking of the fast.

Cultural awareness is important. It helps us understand each other. We can appreciate people from other cultures better when we know a bit about their culture.

There is more to know about the cultures of Saudi Arabia, Israel and Iran. Research and have fun!

Made in the USA
Lexington, KY
21 September 2016